Silly billy

time out

bang on the door™©

Silly billy

time out

First published in 2003 in Great Britain
by HarperCollins*Publishers* Ltd.

1 3 5 7 9 8 6 4 2

ISBN: 0-00-715209-4

Text © 2003 HarperCollins*Publishers* Ltd/Kate Petty

A CIP catalogue record for this title
is available from the British Library.

The HarperCollins website address is: www.**fire**and**water**.com

Printed and bound in Great Britain by Clays Ltd, St Ives plc.

CHAPTER ONE

Have you ever met Silly Billy?

No? Well, you probably have a good friend just like him. Someone who wears odd socks. . . or sunglasses when the sun isn't shining.

Someone who eats chips and ice cream at the same time. Someone who makes everyone laugh – but not ALWAYS on purpose.

Who else lives in Silly Billy's house at Number Six Fool Green, Sunnyvale?

Well, there's his mum, Mrs Billy, who works as a nurse at Sunnyvale Health Centre.

There's his dad, Mr Billy, who's the caretaker at Sunnyvale Primary – Silly Billy's school. That can sometimes be embarrassing!

And then there's his little sister, Daisy. Daisy thinks Silly Billy is brilliant. Even when he's being silly.

Oh, and we mustn't forget about Silly Billy's pets. They are very important members of the Billy family.

Hedgehog is a dog. He thinks that Silly Billy's silliness can be very tiring.

Baz is a rabbit. He doesn't think much at all.

This is a story about the time Silly Billy had a new watch. Silly Billy had chosen his watch from the catalogue. He'd saved up his birthday money and sent off for it.

Then one morning a delivery van
brought a great big parcel.

In the middle of the great big parcel was a beautiful little box, and in the beautiful little box lay Silly Billy's fantastic watch.

"Wow!" said Silly Billy. It was even better than in the catalogue.

It was a very special watch and it could do everything. It had an alarm with a choice of alarm calls to wake Silly Billy up in the morning. It could be used as a stopwatch.

It worked under water.

It could do sums and all sorts of clever things. It could even tell you what time it was in other parts of the world.

The trouble was, Silly Billy wasn't really very good at telling the time in his own part of the world.

That could sometimes be a problem.

CHAPTER TWO

On cold mornings Silly Billy found it hard to get up. He preferred to stay in his nice warm bed. Every day the whole family rushed around before school.

"Oh Silly Billy," said Mrs Billy, "why won't you get up earlier? It would be so nice NOT to rush around for once."

Every day Mr Billy took Silly Billy in the car with him to Sunnyvale Primary.

"Oh Silly Billy," said Mr Billy, "why can't you be ready to leave on time for once? It would be so nice to get to school BEFORE the bell goes."

"All right," said Silly Billy. "Can do!
I'll set the alarm on my new watch."
"Your watch is really brilliant,
Silly Billy," said Daisy.

At bedtime Silly Billy set his watch. He waved his wrist around. He tapped the watch face. He pushed a few buttons.

"That should fix it," said Silly Billy. "Tomorrow morning I'll be ready before any of you." He set the alarm for seven o'clock — or so he thought...

"Whee!" shrieked the referee's whistle. "Whee!" Except it wasn't a referee's whistle – it was the alarm on Silly Billy's fantastic watch.

Silly Billy was still half-asleep.
He waved his wrist around. He bashed
the watch face. He frantically pushed
a few buttons.

At last the whistling alarm stopped. Silly Billy sat up. "That's funny," he thought. "It's still dark." He looked hard at his watch. The long hand was pointing straight up, but the short hand was pointing at the . . . SIX!

SILLY Silly Billy!

Did Silly Billy turn over and go back to sleep? No he didn't. "Oh well," he said to himself. "Now I'm awake I think I'll have some breakfast." He climbed out of bed. "Brr!" It was cold. Silly Billy shivered in his pyjamas.

He couldn't see his dressing gown, so he pulled his school sweatshirt on over his pyjama top.

But he was still cold.

Silly Billy pulled his trousers on over his pyjama bottoms. Then he stepped into his slippers and crept downstairs.

CHAPTER THREE

Silly Billy pushed open the kitchen door. Creeeaaak. Hedgehog the dog came over and sniffed him.

"It's all right, Hedgehog," said Silly Billy. "It's only me. I'm not a burglar."

Hedgehog sighed and went back
to his basket for another snooze.

"Now for some cereal," said
Silly Billy. Hmm. There was a big
pack of Weetcrunchos, Silly Billy's
favourite.

"Whmpf," whimpered Hedgehog.

"All right, Hedgehog," said Silly Billy, and fetched the pack of Doggy Treats. He put them on the table.

"Milk," thought Silly Billy. As he was getting the milk out of the fridge he spotted a bottle of fizzy drink.

"I'm never allowed fizzy drinks for breakfast," thought Silly Billy. "I'll have this now while no one's around. And I'll give it a good shake to make sure it's extra fizzy."

He shook the bottle.

Then he opened the bottle.

OH NO! Fizz squirted everywhere!
SILLY Silly Billy!

Silly Billy wiped himself down and carried on getting his breakfast.

"Bowl and spoon," he remembered. He put them on the table.

"Toast," thought Silly Billy, and put two pieces of bread in the toaster. "And marmalade."

"Whmpf?" whimpered Hedgehog, more urgently. He wanted some of those biscuits NOW.

"All RIGHT, Hedgehog," Silly Billy said crossly, frowning at the dog instead of looking at the label on the jar. It said PICKLE.

Hedgehog wagged his tail and snuffled happily as Silly Billy poured some Weetcrunchos into his bowl.

And then, Silly Billy was VERY Silly.
He tipped some Doggy Treats into his
own bowl and poured milk on them!

CHING! Before Silly Billy had time to tuck in, the toast popped up. So Silly Billy put the toast on a plate, spread butter on the toast and then. . .

spread PICKLE on top!

"I'm hungry!" said Silly Billy, and plunged his spoon into his bowl. . . "PPPPtpth!" Silly Billy was chewing on DOG BISCUITS!

SILLY Silly Billy!

Silly Billy put his bowl down for Hedgehog. "Never mind," he thought. "I've got a nice piece of toast and marmalade to eat." He took a large bite.

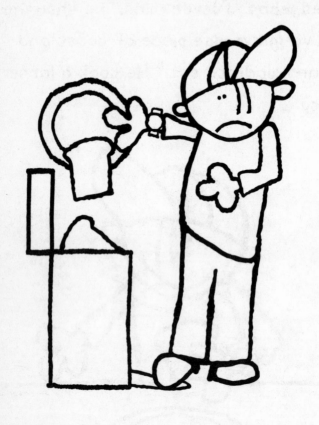

"YUK!" said Silly Billy. He tipped the toast into the rubbish. "And I was so hungry!" he said.

He saw a banana sitting in the fruit bowl and ate that. You can't go far wrong with a banana.

CHAPTER FOUR

It was still only half past six. No one else was up yet.

"I know," said Silly Billy. "I'll do my own packed lunch today to make up for having a horrible breakfast."

He found his yellow lunch box. Mum had already put an apple and a chocolate biscuit in there.

Silly Billy knew what he was going to have in his packed lunch today. Something he never had usually. . . ICE CREAM!

Silly Billy opened the freezer. There was his favourite chocolate-cookie ice cream.

"Why doesn't Mum ever give me this?" wondered Silly Billy, spooning ice cream into a sandwich bag.

Then he saw a big bag of his most favourite food of all. CHIPS!

"Brilliant," cheered Silly Billy. And he put a whole handful of frozen chips into his lunch box. "They'll be

unfrozen by lunch time," he thought.
Silly Billy happily closed the lid of his
yellow lunch box. SNAP. It had the
perfect lunch inside.

Silly Billy could hear Mum and Dad
and Daisy getting up. Wouldn't Mum
be pleased!

Silly Billy thought of all the things he usually had to do before school in the morning. He had to read to Mum or Dad from his reading book.

He had to find something for Show and Tell.

He had to find his PE kit on the
days he had PE.

He had to practise his recorder.

Daisy came downstairs while
Silly Billy was practising his recorder.
TOOTLE TOOT.

"Play *Baa Baa Black Sheep* for me,"
asked Daisy. Silly Billy played *Baa Baa
Black Sheep*.

"Play *Mary had a Little Lamb*," asked Daisy. Silly Billy played *Mary had a Little Lamb*. Daisy knew all the words.

"What should I take for Show and Tell, Daisy?" asked Silly Billy.

"You should take an animal," said Daisy, dreamily.

"Now THAT'S a good idea," said Silly Billy. He picked up his school bag and went out into the garden.

"Baz?" he called. "Baz, how would you like to come to school with me?" Silly Billy put some comfortable straw in his bag. He put Baz's water bowl in his bag. He put a handful of rabbit food in his bag.

And then he put BAZ in his bag. . .
Baz sighed and went back to sleep.

"Silly Billy!" called Mrs Billy. "You've
got time to read to me this morning.
Find your reading book."

Silly Billy looked for his reading book. "There it is!" cried Silly Billy at last, and sat down with Mrs Billy to read. It was an exciting story, and Silly Billy read right to the end.

Mr Billy listened to the story too.
Right to the end. Then he looked at
the clock. "Goodness me, is that the
time?" he said. "Come on, Silly Billy, we
need to be off!"

"I've got my lunch," said Silly Billy. "And I've got something for Show and Tell."

He pointed at his bag, which looked large and lumpy and moved a little. "And I've got my reading book."

"Is it PE today?" asked Mrs Billy.
"Yes, I nearly forgot," said Silly Billy.
There were two carrier bags hanging on the pegs. Silly Billy grabbed the one with his PE kit in it.

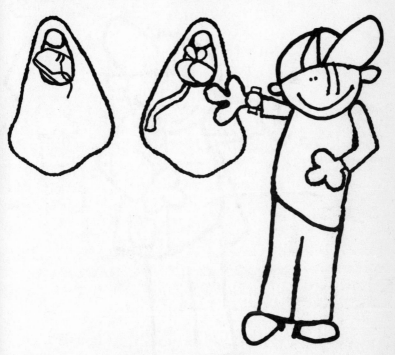

At least, he THOUGHT it was his PE kit.

He put on his coat and shoes and off he went to school with his dad. But Silly Billy had forgotten about something else...

CHAPTER FIVE

Silly Billy put his lunch box on the windowsill with all the other lunch boxes. The sun was shining through the window.

He hung up his coat and his PE kit and went into the classroom.

"Who's got something for Show and Tell this morning?" asked Miss Sweet, the teacher, once the children had settled.

"I have!" said Silly Billy, quick as a flash. He opened his bag and... out hopped BAZ! Hippity hoppity went Baz all around the classroom.

"SILLY Silly Billy!" exclaimed Miss Sweet. "We'll have to call the caretaker at once." Silly Billy blushed. He wasn't looking forward to his dad, the caretaker, seeing Baz one bit.

Mr Billy, arrived and took Baz
from Silly Billy. "SILLY Silly Billy,"
he said. "It wasn't very kind to take
Baz to school."

"I made sure he was comfortable,"
said Silly Billy.

"I'll take the rabbit home at once,"
said Mr Billy to Miss Sweet. "And by
the way, I noticed that somebody's
lunch box was dripping as I came by."

"I wonder whose that could be?"
said Miss Sweet.

"I'll fetch it," said Mr Billy.

Miss Sweet held up a yellow lunch
box. Silly Billy recognised it straight
away, but he didn't say anything. He
felt too silly.

Miss Sweet opened the lunch box
and saw that it was full of melted
ice cream and raw, soggy chips.

"I know whose lunch box that is," said Mr Billy.

SILLY Silly Billy.

"I'll sort out a proper packed lunch when I take the rabbit back," said Mr Billy.

"Never mind, Silly Billy," said Miss Sweet. "It's time to change for PE now. We're going outside to practise for sports day."

CHAPTER SIX

Silly Billy and his friends went to change into their PE kits.

Silly Billy put his hand into his shoebag, but instead of his trainers he pulled out a pair of PINK BALLET SHOES!

And then, instead of his T-shirt, he pulled out a PINK LEOTARD!

And next, instead of his shorts, he pulled out a PINK TUTU!

POOR Silly Billy! He'd taken Daisy's bag instead of his own.

"Never mind, Silly Billy," said Miss Sweet. She was feeling quite sorry for Silly Billy. "I'm sure we can find you something to wear. Take off your sweatshirt and trousers while I look in the cupboard."

So Silly Billy took off his sweatshirt
and trousers.
Everybody gasped.

Then everybody laughed. Even
Silly Billy. He was still wearing his
PYJAMAS!

"Quieten down, everyone," said Miss Sweet turning away from the cupboard. "I've found some spare kit for Silly Billy. But unfortunately I can't find the stopwatch for our races."

Then she saw Silly Billy. "Goodness
Silly Billy," she said. "Whatever
happened to you today?"

"It all started because of my fantastic watch," said Silly Billy.

"Fantastic watch?" questioned Miss Sweet. "Does it have a stopwatch on it?"

"Of course!" said Silly Billy proudly.

"You've saved the day, Silly Billy,"
said Miss Sweet.

Then Mr Billy arrived back with Silly Billy's lunch box with a fresh lunch in it. He also had Silly Billy's PE kit.

Silly Billy ran off to change.

When he came back he waved his wrist around.

He tapped the watch face.

He pushed a few buttons.

He handed his fantastic stopwatch
to Miss Sweet and went to join in
the races.

And he even won one, too!

silly billy

The characters in this book were
played by:

silly billy	himself
Mr Billy	'handyman'
Mrs Billy	'mum'
Daisy Billy	'fun in the sun'
Mrs Sweet	'lovely'
Hedgehog	'puppy'
Referee	'dad'
Baz	'rabbit'

bang on the door™ ©

silly billy

**Read the next adventure of Silly Billy —
the silliest boy in the WHOLE world.**

POOL FOOL

Silly Billy can't wait to get to school
today. It's swimming class this morning,
and he loves to splash around in the pool.
But he's forgotten to bring something
VERY important...
And what IS Silly Billy doing with
those armbands?

Collins

An imprint of HarperCollins*Publishers*

bang on the door ™ ©

drama queen
Drama Queen makes a drama out of
EVERYTHING. Read about her
latest adventure in . . .

STAGE STRUCK

Drama Queen is very excited!
She loves to dance and sing and act
and she is desperate to be Snow White
in the school play.
But will she get the part?
And who will play Prince Charming?

Collins

An imprint of HarperCollins*Publishers*

bang on the door™ ©

friends

Together we make things happen!

Meet Spex, Jude, Tiger,
Sugar, Spice, Flash and Cookie.
Follow their adventures as
they set up a newspaper and
report on crimes, local issues
and Tiger's mum's cooking!

FRIENDS
The Friends set up the *Sunnyvale Standard* to
fight the plans of a dastardly property developer.

FRIENDS UNITED
Disaster! The local pool has been closed down –
and just before the summer hols! It's a race
against time as the Friends swing into action
to save their pool.

And coming soon...

FRIENDS AGAIN
The Friends discover local animals are in danger
and tempers are running high. Can they pull
together... and catch the culprit?

An imprint of HarperCollinsPublishers

bang on the door™ ©

poo jokebook
Every pun is guaranteed to pong
in this stinky collection!

What do you get if you cross an
elephant with a bottle of laxative?
Out of the way!

What do you get if you eat baked
beans and onions?
Tear gas!

Packed with wicked whiffs, real stinkers and
nasty niffs – jokes that will run and run!

An imprint of HarperCollinsPublishers

bang on the door™ ©

Collect 5 tokens and get a free poster!*

All you have to do is collect five funky tokens!
You can snip one from any of these cool Bang on the Door books!

0 00 715209 4

0 00 715309 0

0 00 715212 4

0 00 715210 8

Send 5 tokens with a completed coupon to: Bang on the Door Poster Offer

PO Box 142, Horsham, RH13 5FJ (UK residents)

c/- HarperCollins Publishers (NZ) Ltd,
PO Box 1, Auckland (NZ residents)

c/- HarperCollins Publishers, PO Box 321,
Pymble NSW 2073, Australia
(for Australian residents)

0 00 715220 5

- -

First name: .... Surname: ....

Address: ....

....

....

Postcode: .... Child's date of birth: .... / .... / ....

email address: ....

Signature of parent/guardian: ....

Tick here if you do not wish to receive further information about children's books ☐

SB1

1 token

Terms and Conditions: Proof of sending cannot be considered proof of receipt.
Not redeemable for cash. Please allow 28 days for delivery. Photocopied tokens not accepted.
Offer open to UK, New Zealand and Australia only while stocks last.*rrp £3.99